Frogs & Toads

Tamara Einstein &
Einstein Sisters

KidsWorld

Frogs

Waxy Monkey Tree Frog

All frogs are
amphibians. They are
carnivores, which means
they eat other animals, such
as insects and worms. Frogs
can be colorful, but most
frogs are green
or brown.

Frogs usually have smooth, shiny skin, large mouths, big eyes and powerful hind legs. Frogs live either in freshwater or in humid forests.

Northern Leopard Frog

More than 4700 species of frogs and toads have been discovered.

Toads

Toads are
a type of frog. They
have bumpy skin.
Toads are mainly found
on land, but they
mate and lay eggs
in water.

European Green Toad

Common Toad

Toads have drier
skin than other frogs,
and their legs are shorter.
Because of their short legs,
toads are not as good at
jumping as frogs.

Amphibians

Frogs and toads are amphibians. All amphibians are vertebrates, which means they have backbones and skeletons. Amphibians are cold-blooded animals, so their body temperature changes as the air temperature changes.

Narayan's Caecilian

Caecilians are legless amphibians. They are snake-like, but are not related to snakes.

California Tiger Salamander

Salamanders and newts look like lizards, but they are also amphibians. Salamanders and newts are capable of regrowing lost legs, eyes, jaws and even tails!

California Newt

Amphibians start life as larvae. The larvae have gills to breathe underwater. When they undergo metamorphosis, they transform into adults with lungs.

Groups

A bunch of frogs in a group is called an **army** of frogs.

A group
of many toads is
called a knot
of toads.

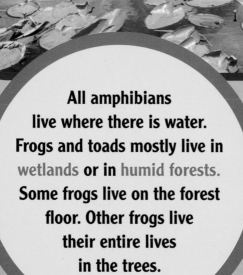

All amphibians
live where there is water.
Frogs and toads mostly live in
wetlands or in humid forests.
Some frogs live on the forest
floor. Other frogs live
their entire lives
in the trees.

Frogs and toads are found on every continent except Antarctica. Tropical rainforests **have more different kinds of frogs.**

Life Cycle

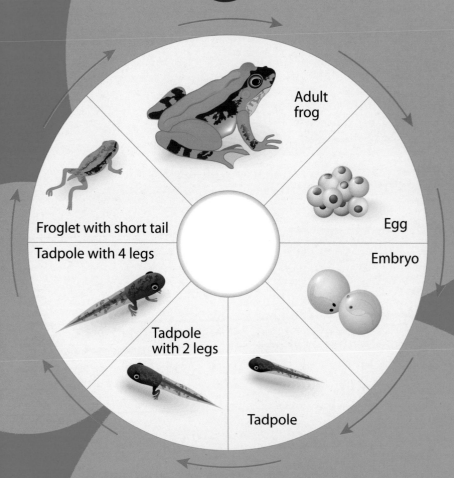

A life cycle refers to the stages that an animal goes through while it is alive. The life cycle of a frog has many stages.

A frog's life starts as an egg. The embryo develops and hatches into a tadpole. The tadpole then undergoes **metamorphosis** to become an adult frog. Female frogs lay eggs to begin the cycle again.

Metamorphosis is a fast and major change in body structure.

Eggs

Frog Eggs

Frogs and toads can produce from a few eggs to many thousands. One female American bullfrog can lay as many as 20,000 eggs!

Frog Eggs

Toad Eggs

Toad Eggs

Frogs eggs are always in a clump. Toads mostly lay eggs in strands.

Bubble Nests

Many frogs
make bubble nests
Eggs are held in a clump
and attached to leaves with
foam. When the eggs hatch,
the tadpoles drop into
the water below.

Bromeliads are plants that grow on other plants. Tree frogs often lay their eggs in the water that collects in the centre of the bromeliad.

Bromeliads

Ground Nests

Hill Forest Frog

Some frogs make nests on the ground. These nest look like small pools near the edge of water. Pool nests help to protect the eggs from predation by fish and other aquatic predators. Limborg's frog and the hill forest frog are two species that make these little nests.

Limborg's Frog

The Vizcacheras' white-lipped frog builds one of the most unusual frog nests. The male makes a volcano-shaped mud nest. Then the female comes to lay her eggs in the mud nest. The male protects the nest while the eggs develop.

Vizcacheras' White-lipped Frog

Glass Frog

Protecting Eggs

Female glass frogs lay their eggs in a clump stuck to a leaf. Males have white spots on their backs that resemble a clump of eggs. When hungry wasps come to eat the eggs, the male swiftly kicks them away. One sting from the wasp could kill the frog, but he stays put to defend the eggs.

Common Midwife Toad

A male common midwife toad carries eggs laid by the female on his back. He winds the strands of eggs around his back and hind legs. If the eggs start to dry out, he goes for a swim. When they are ready to hatch, he releases the tadpoles into a pool of water.

Embedded Eggs

The common Suriname toad has perhaps one of the weirdest ways to protect its eggs. This toad looks nearly flat and lives almost entirely underwater.

Common Suriname Toad

Common Suriname Toad

The female lays eggs that are distributed over her back by the male. She grows a special thin layer of skin over the eggs to protect them. After the tadpoles have developed, the tiny froglets emerge. The female then sheds the protective layer of skin.

Swallowing Eggs

Gastric-brooding Frog

The gastric-brooding frog was the only frog known to swallow its own eggs into its stomach. After the female swallowed her eggs, her normal digestion stopped. The eggs hatched in her stomach, and the tadpoles developed. After a few weeks, the froglets emerged from her mouth. There were two species of these frogs in Australia. Neither has been seen for many years. They are now considered extinct.

Darwin's Frog

Darwin's frog is a living frog that also swallows its eggs. Females lay their eggs in leaf litter, and the males guard them.

Once the embryos in the eggs start to move, the male swallows them and holds them in his vocal sacs. The tadpoles hatch and develop in his vocal sacs for 6 weeks until they are froglets. They then hop out of his mouth.

Tadpoles

When an embryo hatches from an egg, it is called a tadpole.

Tadpoles are also called pollywogs. Tadpoles are the larval stage of amphibians that live freely in freshwater. They have gills for breathing. Tadpoles feed mainly on plants and grow quickly.

Tadpoles tend to stay in groups for safety. They also prefer shallow, warm water.

As they grow, the tadpole's tail shrinks and its legs develop.

Protecting Tadpoles

Sky Blue Dart Frog

Many dart frogs lay their eggs on leaves in the rainforest. When the eggs hatch, the male carries the tadpoles on his back. He takes them to water that has collected in a bromeliad plant.

In the water of a bromeliad plant the tadpoles develop into frogs. They feed on bits of plants. Sometimes the female lays infertile eggs for the tadpoles to eat.

Froglets and Toadlets

When tadpoles have all four legs and they come out of the water, they are called froglets or toadlets. Froglets still have tails. Their tails are absorbed as they become adults.

The transformation of a tadpole into a frog is complex. The mouth becomes much wider, the lungs develop, the intestines shorten and the legs grow. This rapid change is called metamorphosis.

Direct Development

Cuzco Robber Frog

Some species of frogs do not undergo metamorphosis. The embryos in the eggs develop into fully-formed tiny frogs. This is called direct development.

Solomon Island Leaf Frog

Direct development means that the frogs skip the underwater tadpole stage. Some frogs that develop directly, such as the Solomon island leaf frog, live in the forest and never go into water.

Solomon Island Leaf Frog

Live Birth

Nimbaphrynoides occidentalis

A few species of frogs skip egg-laying altogether. *Nimbaphrynoides occidentalis* is a species that lives in west Africa. Females don't lay eggs. Instead, the eggs develop inside her abdomen, and she gives birth to fully formed froglets.

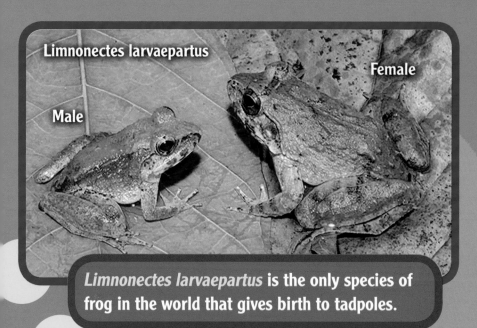

Limnonectes larvaepartus

Male

Female

Limnonectes larvaepartus is the only species of frog in the world that gives birth to tadpoles.

The eggs develop inside the female. When ready, she gives birth to the tadpoles into a slow-moving stream.

Tadpoles

Anatomy

Students often use frogs students to learn about **anatomy**. Even though frogs are amphibians, their bodies and organs are similar to other animals, including humans.

Frogs may be used for dissection. They are cut open so students can study their internal organs.

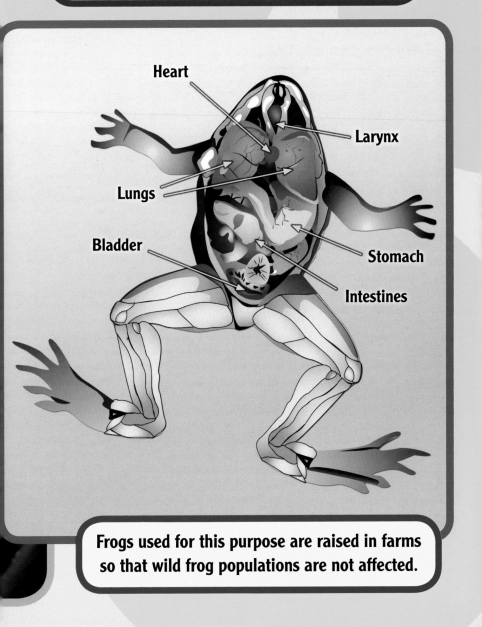

Heart

Larynx

Lungs

Bladder

Stomach

Intestines

Frogs used for this purpose are raised in farms so that wild frog populations are not affected.

Eating

Feae's Flying Frog

Frogs cannot take bites of their food. They can only eat creatures that will fit in their mouths whole. Most frogs eat insects, caterpillars, worms and other invertebrates.

Frogs can also eat other frogs. Large frogs, such as **bullfrogs**, eat smaller species of frogs.

American Bullfrog

Tongue

Most frogs use their long, sticky tongues to catch their prey. They can shoot their tongues out at great speed. A frog's tongue can snap back into its mouth in a fraction of a second.

African Bullfrog

Common Toad

The long tongue is coiled in the frog's mouth when not in use.

Teeth

Green Frog

Although we don't think of frogs having teeth, they actually do! Frogs have tiny teeth in their upper jaws that help hold their prey. Frogs do lose their teeth and grow new ones during their lives. Toads do not have any teeth.

Teeth

A frog's tiny teeth can be seen on this skeleton.

Fanged Frog

Fanged frogs have large teeth on their lower jaws to help hold their prey.

Ears

Frogs and toads have good hearing. The ear is marked by a circular patch behind the eye. The circle is the frog's eardrum.

American Bullfrog

Eardrum

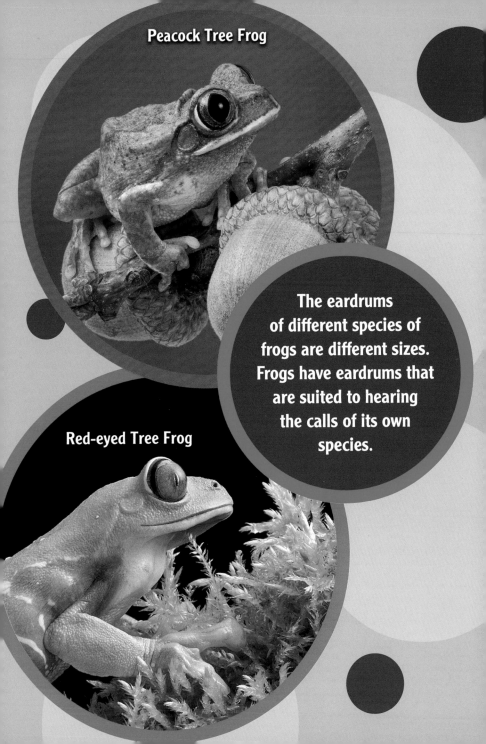

Peacock Tree Frog

Red-eyed Tree Frog

The eardrums of different species of frogs are different sizes. Frogs have eardrums that are suited to hearing the calls of its own species.

Eyes

Peacock Tree Frog

Günther's Bush Frog

Frogs have large eyes and excellent vision. Because most frogs eat insects that fly, jump or run, they need good vision to catch their prey.

Frogs have eyelids and can completely close their eyes. They also have transparent inner eyelids. The inner eyelid can be closed to protect the eye while still allowing the frog to see.

Red-eyed Tree Frog

Common Toad

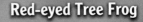

Red-eyed Tree Frog

The pupil is the dark center of the eye. Most frogs have either horizontal or vertical pupils. The tomato frog has round pupils, and the yellow-bellied toad has pupils shaped like a heart!

Tomato Frog

Yellow-bellied Toad

Frogs use their eyeballs for swallowing! Their eyeballs draw back into their heads to help push food down their throats.

Skin

American Bullfrog

Frogs and toads can breathe through their skin! Their skin can also absorb water so they don't need to drink.

Special glands on a frog's skin keep the skin moist. The skin is also slippery, helping them to better escape predators! The glands of some frogs and toads produce toxins, making them poisonous.

Some frogs have skin that can change color.

Cane Toad Skin

Toes

Red-eyed Tree Frog

Frogs that live in trees have long toes with sticky pads. Tree frogs are acrobatic. They can hang from just one toe!

Webbed Feet

Frogs and toads that spend some or all of their lives in water have webbed feet.

European Common Frog

Webbed feet act like flippers, helping the frog to swim fast.

African Dwarf Frog

Some frogs, like the African dwarf frog, have webbed front feet. These frogs live completely underwater. They come to the surface to breathe.

Webbed Hind Foot

Feet for Digging

Spadefoot toads have special feet that help them dig. "Spade" is another word for shovel. These toads have a hard ridge along their hind feet so they can dig backwards into the ground.

Western Spadefoot Toad

Turtle Frog

The turtle frog in Australia and the purple frog in India both live most of their lives underground, feeding on termites. Both frogs have short, muscular legs and feet to help them dig. Turtle frogs dig forward into the sand, while purple frogs dig backward.

Purple Frog

Swimming

Most frogs and toads are excellent swimmers. They have strong hind legs and webbed feet to push them through the water.

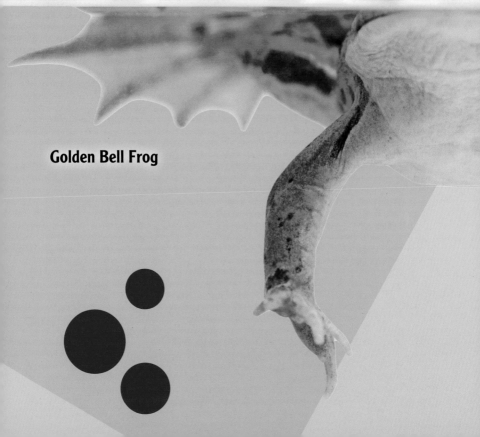

Golden Bell Frog

American Bullfrog

Frogs such as tree frogs and dart frogs almost never go into water. They can still swim if they need to.

Flying Frogs

Flying frogs? **Yes! Webbed feet are useful for more than just swimming. A few kinds of tree frogs have long, fully webbed toes on all four feet. This webbing helps the frogs "fly" from tree to tree.**

Wallace's Flying Frog

Wallace's Flying Frog

Flying frogs **cannot fly the same way birds fly. They glide. Flying frogs leap into the air and stretch their toes out. They can glide for about 15 meters (50 feet), a distance longer than a school bus!**

Jumping

Compared to their size, frogs are the best jumpers of all vertebrates. The striped rocket frog is the size of an apricot, and it can leap more than 2 metres (6.5 feet). That distance is more than fifty times its body length!

Striped Rocket Frog

Frogs jump to escape predators and to catch prey.

Horned Frog

Croaking

Marsh Frog

Frogs and toads make croaking sounds to communicate with each other. Most frogs have vocal sacs that fill with air. The air is moved through the throat to make the sound. The sound echoes in the vocal sacs and becomes louder. Some frogs have two vocal sacs, while others have only one.

Marsh Frog

European Tree Frog

American Toad

Males croak to attract females. If a frog is in water, the vibration of the sound produces a pattern of waves on the surface.

Each type of frog makes a croak unique to its species.

Banded Bullfrog

Predation

Many animals eat frogs. Many predators also eat the frog's eggs and tadpoles. Frogs mainly rely on camouflage and jumping to avoid getting caught by predators.

Snakes, skunks, birds and raccoons regularly eat frogs.

Sleeping

Red-eyed Tree Frog

We don't know for sure if frogs sleep the way people do. Frogs definitely rest and close their eyes.

Common Tree Frog

When resting, frogs tuck in their feet and stay motionless.

Glass Frogs

Yellow-spotted Burrowing Frog

Frogs that live in warm climates may have to survive long dry seasons. Some frogs, like the yellow-spotted burrowing frog in Australia, bury themselves in mud for many months until the rains return. This kind of hibernation is called estivation.

Frozen Frog

While it may sound impossible, some frogs survive the winter by letting themselves freeze!

Wood frogs and chorus frogs live in parts of North America where winters are cold and snowy. These frogs bury themselves under leaves and mud or hide under logs. Their bodies have sugary antifreeze to keep their organs from freezing. These frogs can freeze and thaw several times during the winter, and in spring they thaw completely!

Wood Frog

Frog in Snow

Hibernation

Camouflage

Camouflaged Frog

Grey Tree Frog

Most frogs and toads use camouflage to help hide themselves from predators. Some frogs have such good camouflage that they are almost impossible to see!

Asian Horned Frog

Mossy Frog

Frogs also use camouflage to confuse their prey. Camouflaged frogs stay motionless as they wait for their prey to approach. They then lunge forward to capture the prey with their tongues or mouths.

Warning Colors

Poison dart frogs are some of the most colorful of all frogs. These frogs secrete a poisonous toxin from their skin. Their bright colors serve as a warning to predators not to eat them.

Golden Dart Frog

Red-backed Dart Frog

Blue Dart Frog

Strawberry Dart Frog

Variable Dart Frog

Yellow-banded Dart Frog

Dart frogs get their name because the Indigenous people of South America would rub the tips of their blowdarts on the backs of these frogs to make their blowdarts deadly. Only four species of dart frogs are toxic enough to be used for poison darts.

Defense

Many animals eat frogs. Frogs and toads have developed many ways to defend themselves from predators. Camouflage is an excellent defense, but many frogs use other methods as well.

Tomato Frog

The tomato frog puffs itself up and secretes a toxin that numbs the mouth and eyes of a predator.

Common Toad

The common toad rises up on its legs to make itself look big and threatening.

Yellow-bellied Toad

Some frogs, such as this yellow-bellied toad, play dead when they are afraid. Many predators avoid eating dead things.

Glow-in-the-Dark Frogs

The polka-dot tree frog is the first amphibian discovered that glows in the dark. Both males and females glow, and the frogs can see the glow. Researchers think the glow helps with communication and mating.

Polka-dot Tree Frog

During the day, the polka-dot tree frog is green with red spots. At night, it glows blue with dark spots.

Changing Colors

Some frogs can change colors. The grey tree frog changes color depending on where it sits. On bark it will be grey. On leaves it will be green. On purple berries it will be nearly black!

Grey Tree Frog

Painted Reed Frog

During the day, painted reed frogs are drab and pale. At night, they are brightly colored and marbled!

During mating season, male Indian Bullfrogs turn bright yellow and inflate their blue vocal sacs.

Indian Bullfrog

Transparent Frogs

Glass Frog

Glass frogs are a group of frogs that live mainly in Central America. Females lay their eggs in trees above water. Males protect the eggs until they hatch, and the tadpoles fall into the water below.

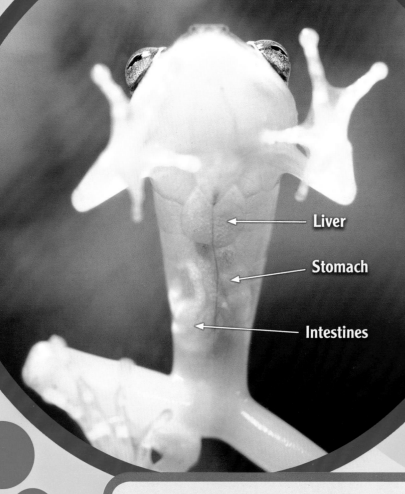

Glass frogs have green backs, but their undersides are transparent!

Liver

Stomach

Intestines

Because their skin is transparent, you can see a glass frog's internal organs. See here its liver, stomach and intestines!

Largest and Smallest

Paedophryne amauensis

The smallest frog in the world lives in New Guinea, an island near Australia. At only 7 or 8 millimeters long (0.3 inches), this frog is also the smallest vertebrate in the world. Its name is *Paedophryne amauensis* Here it is sitting on a dime.

The largest frog in the world is the Goliath frog. This frog is found only in a small part of west-central Africa. It can grow to more than 30 centimeters (1 foot) long—not including its legs!

Goliath Frog

Frogs as Pets

Some frogs are kept as pets. Frogs need a glass tank with plants, water and bugs to eat. This kind of tank is called a vivarium.

Red-backed Dart Frog

Red-eyed Tree Frog

Argentine Horned Frog

Most pet frogs hatch from eggs laid by other pet frogs. In order to protect wild frogs, it is important never to buy frogs taken from the wild or collect them.

Problem Frogs

Cane Toad

Cane toads have been introduced to many islands and countries because they eat large numbers of cockroaches and other pest insects. These toads, however, also eat many other species and can cause native animals to decline. Cane toads also produce a toxin on their skin that can kill animals that eat them.

American bullfrogs are farmed as food and have been introduced into many countries and to parts of the United States where there were none before. Escaped bullfrogs quickly reproduce and eat large numbers of other frogs, fish, birds, rodents and reptiles. They also spread disease that can kill other species of frogs.

American Bullfrog

Frogs in Your Garden

Some frogs live happily in backyards and gardens. Having frogs in your garden can help reduce the number of pest insects on your plants. This means you don't have to use chemicals to kill harmful insects.

Frogs and toads can eat dozens of insects each day. Providing places for frogs to hide and water for them to sit in will increase their numbers in your garden.

Eating Frogs

People in many cultures around the world eat frogs. Usually it is just the hindlegs that are eaten.

Some kinds of frogs are farmed for food. Other frogs are taken from the wild. When wild frogs are caught and eaten, the species may decline in number.

Would you eat frog's legs?

Decline of Frogs

Most frogs around the world are declining in numbers. The main reason for their decline is habitat loss and water pollution.

Other reasons for decline include predation by introduced species and disease. The most dangerous disease is a fungus that damages their skin and kills them.

Myths

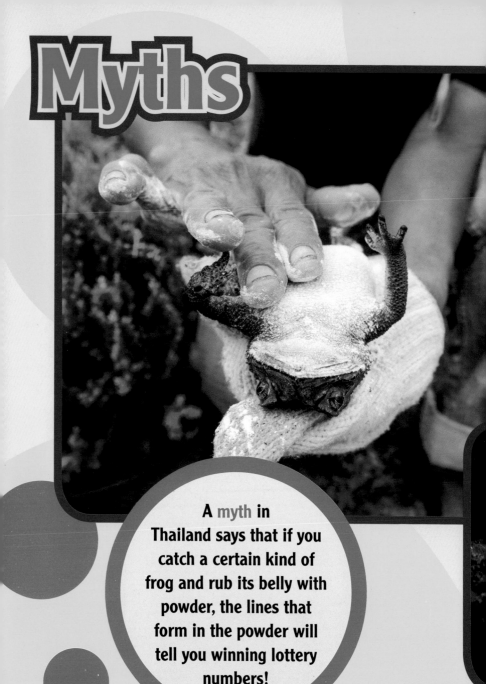

A myth in Thailand says that if you catch a certain kind of frog and rub its belly with powder, the lines that form in the powder will tell you winning lottery numbers!

Of course, we all know that kissing a frog won't turn it into a prince. But many people believe that touching a toad will give you warts. Even though toads look like they have warts, warts on a human are caused by a virus that has nothing to do with toads!

The Publisher: KidsWorld Books

Library and Archives Canada Cataloguing in Publication

Title: Frogs & toads / Tamara Einstein & Einstein Sisters.
Other titles: Frogs and toads
Names: Einstein, Tamara, author. | Einstein Sisters, author.
Identifiers: Canadiana (print) 20190053992 | Canadiana (ebook) 20190054018 | ISBN 9781988183428 (softcover) | ISBN 9781988183435 (EPUB)
Subjects: LCSH: Frogs—Juvenile literature. | LCSH: Toads—Juvenile literature. | LCSH: Frogs—Miscellanea—Juvenile literature. | LCSH: Toads—Miscellanea—Juvenile literature.
Classification: LCC QL668.E2 E46 2019 | DDC j597.8/9—dc23

Book Layout: Tamara Hartson

Cover Design: Greg Brown, Tamara Hartson

Front cover: From Getty Images, kikkerdirk/aga7ta.

Back cover: From Getty Images, Jrleyland, BrianLasenby, ABDESIGN.

Photo credits: From Getty Images: 1stGallery 46a; 3quarks 26; ABDESIGN 81; alekseystemmer 84-85; Anant_Kasetsinsombut 66b; Andy-Holt 52-53; Arndt_Vladimir 27a; Azureus70 72c; blueringmedia 13; BrianEKushner 65a; BrianLasenby 42-43; CathyKeifer 2, 3, 45a, 45b; Chris Leaver 89b; Christian Sorensen 47a; Claudio Arriagada 25; CreativeNature_nl 8, 27b, 62b; davemhuntphotography 5, 71b; DavidovArt 69b; DebraLee Wiseberg 17a; Denise Erickson 54a; dimid_86 49; ePhotocorp 31b; Farinosa 38; fazon1 92; freebilly 36; GCHaggisImages 68a; Ginette Leclair 44; Goldfinch4ever 15b, 30; hfoxfoto 47d; hypergurl 50b; Ian_Redding 15a; icestylecg 89a; ichimabi 37; Igor Krasilov 65b; IliasStrachinis 87; Image Source 95; Ja'Crispy/aloke1984tw 61b; JAH 41a; jamcgraw 85a; Jupiterimages 39a; KeithSzafranski 70b; kerkla 66a; Kevin Wells 46c; kikkerdirk 28-29, 56-57, 72b, 84a; Linas Toleikis 50a; LuBueno 29b; macro frog insect animal 59-60; Marie-Lise Beaudin 48; MriyaWildlife 62a; mzphoto11 40; NajaShots 85b; NaniP 20a, 20b, 41b; nedomacki 9; NTCo 73a; nui7711 51; Obencem 57a; prill 14; quickshooting 11; reptiles4all 33a, 33b, 73b, 80a; Rixipix 86; romrodinka 10; RosalinaLorien 75b; RussellGr 63a; S.Rohrlach 31a; SHAWSHANK61 73c; tang90246 71a; Thorsten Spoerlein 72a; Toa55 93; TPAP8228 88; TravelStrategy 47b; ttsz 12, 12; udra 90-91; vicnt 63b; Volodymyr Kucherenko 64; Werner Schneider 68b; wichatsurin 94. From Wikimedia Commons: Acatenazzi 32a; Alpsdake 16b; Amanda Santiago F. L. Silva 17b; Bernard DUPONT 79b; Casa Rosada (Argentina Presidency of the Nation) 77b; Chris Brown, USGS 54b; Christian Fischer 21; Connor Long 7b; David Perez 53b; David V. Raju 46b, 55b; Dein Freund der Baum 23b; Djoko T. Iskandar, Ben J. Evans, Jimmy A. McGuire 35a, 35b; Dustykid 78b; Erfil 77a; Franco Andreonejpg 47c; Froggydarb 60; Hugo Claessen 22; John Mather 74; Łukasz Olszewski ImreKiss 75a; Mauricio Rivera Correa 80b; Notafly 43a; Pacific Southwest Region USFWS 7a; Pavel Kirillov 76; Pierre Fidenci 32b; PoojaRathod 16a; Rajan007RJ 79d; Reshma&ashi 70a; Rittmeyer EN, Allison A, Gründler MC, Thompson DK, Austin CC 82; Rushen 19a; Rushenb / Jegelewicz 43b; Rushenb 18, 58a; Sandberger-Loua L, Müller H, Rödel M-O 34; Sandilya Theuerkauf 79c; Sanjay Acharya 67; Slashme 79a; Stan Shebs 23a; Stephen Zozaya 55a; Thomas Jensen (Medical Prognosis Institute, Denmark) 61a; U. S. Fish and Wildlife Service - Northeast Region 69a; Umberto Salvagnin 4; USFWSmidwest 78a; Uspn 39b; Venu Govindappa 6. Sience Source: Michael J. Tyler 24. Other: Chien C. Lee 59a; Christopher M. Schalk 19b; Living Zoology-Matej and Zuzana Dolinay 83.

Tree Frog Illustration: From Getty Images, julos.

We acknowledge the financial support of the Government of Canada.
Nous reconnaissons l'appui financier du gouvernement du Canada.

Funded by the Government of Canada.
Financé par le gouvernement du Canada.